PUFFIN BOOKS

BRIGHT-EYE

Amanda's father thinks it's a waste of time trying to hatch out the wild duck's egg he's saved from the ploughed field; 'I'd say nine times out of ten, nothing comes of it.' But Amanda will not be put off. She is sure this egg is special, and determined it *is* going to hatch out into a lovely little duckling which she can keep as her very own pet!

Bright-Eye is an appealing, warmly written story, told with 'exact and loving observation' – *Times Literary Supplement*

Alison Morgan has been writing since the age of ten. Her first book, *River Song*, was completed during the short gap between giving up teaching and getting married. She has been a teacher, housewife, lecturer, and Justice of the Peace, and has also been involved in short-term fostering and many youth activities. She has two sons and lives in Wales.

Alison Morgan

Bright-Eye

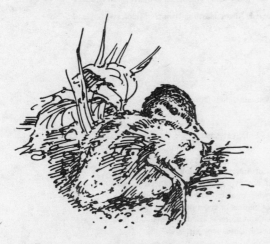

Illustrated by Vanessa Julian-Ottie

PUFFIN BOOKS

To Clare

PUFFIN BOOKS

Published by the Penguin Group
Penguin Books Ltd, 27 Wrights Lane, London W8 5TZ, England
Penguin Books USA Inc., 375 Hudson Street, New York, New York 10014, USA
Penguin Books Australia Ltd, Ringwood, Victoria, Australia
Penguin Books Canada Ltd, 2801 John Street, Markham, Ontario, Canada L3R 1B4
Penguin Books (NZ) Ltd, 182–190 Wairau Road, Auckland 10, New Zealand

Penguin Books Ltd, Registered Offices: Harmondsworth, Middlesex, England

First published by Kestrel Books 1984
Published in Puffin Books 1985
10 9 8 7 6 5 4

Printed in England by Clays Ltd, St Ives plc
Set in Palatino

Chapter One

From where Amanda sat at her table in the classroom she could see just over half the field known as the Rhos. Almost every farm in this part of Wales had a field called the Rhos, which means a rough, marshy place, overgrown with tussocks of reeds, because it is that kind of country. The farmers all complained about the heavy clay soil, which was difficult to drain and meant that all the crops came later, and were thinner and poorer, than those of their neighbours down Hereford way. Amanda's father complained as much as any of them, for it was his field

Amanda was looking at, and he was ploughing it up.

Ah! There it came again, the old blue tractor, bucking slowly along over the rough ground. That was what Amanda was waiting for; it disappeared from her view as it crossed the top of the field to work its way down the next furrow, and then reappeared about three quarters of the way down. Each time it disappeared, Amanda tried to guess when it would come into view again. She never seemed to get it just right. Sometimes it turned up before she expected it, but this time it took longer.

'Amanda! Stop dreaming. Pay attention!'

'Yes, Mrs Davies.' She spoke pertly; the rest of the class laughed, as she knew they would, because Mrs Davies was her mother.

It was difficult at times, having a mother who was your class teacher: you had to be naughty enough to make sure she got cross with you, or your friends would say you were Mummy's pet and turn their backs on you; but not so naughty that the crossness spilled over into home. Amanda felt her mother did not always understand this properly, but most of the time it was all right.

When she got home that afternoon, there was a large egg in a bowl on the kitchen table. It was about the same size as a hen's egg, but a different shape, being more pointed at one end, and it was a soft greenish-brown colour all over.

'Where did this egg come from, Dad?' she asked.

'I thought you might like it for your tea.'

'Where did it come from?'

'Mallard's egg, that is. Wild duck.'

'You're not allowed to take wild birds' eggs,' said Amanda quickly, because she had been told that many times at school. Nor wild flowers. Her mother was very particular about that. Mrs Davies had been brought up in a town and she was a lot more particular about taking care of country things than most of the country people were. More than Dad, for instance.

'Nor I wouldn't have, either,' said Mr Davies. 'Only the plough went right through the nest before I knew anything about it.'

'Oh, what about the mother duck?' cried Amanda.

'She wasn't on the nest, don't you worry. No, it was a new nest, and she hadn't finished laying. There weren't more than three eggs – two were broken, and this one had rolled clear.'

'Still ...' said Amanda. She picked up the egg and felt the weight of it, and its shape and smoothness, in her hand.

'They don't make much of a nest, ducks,' said her father. 'She'll start a new one somewhere else, and lay another clutch of eggs, don't you worry. It's early in the season yet.'

Amanda turned the egg over carefully in her hand. She was used to collecting up the

hens' eggs and was sometimes hasty and let one slip and break, but this egg was special.

'Supposing it's got a baby duckling in it,' she said. 'It will die.'

'It won't have,' said her father. 'They don't start to form inside the egg until the duck starts to sit, and she won't do that till she's laid all she's going to lay – maybe a dozen, even. Otherwise they'd all start to hatch at different times and the first one would be ready to leave the nest before the later ones had hatched.'

'You should know that, Amanda,' said her mother, coming into the room to see the egg. 'We've talked about that in school,' she added, unfairly.

'Yes, but I'm not in school now, am I?' said Amanda, which wasn't sensible, but her mother took the hint.

'Pretty, isn't it?' she said, stroking the greeny-brown egg where it lay nested in Amanda's cupped hand. 'Well, I suppose you may as well have it for tea if you'd like it ... though it doesn't seem quite right,' she added.

'They make good eating, wild duck eggs,' said Mr Davies. 'And plovers' eggs as well.'

'Ssh!' cried Mrs Davies, shocked.

'I've never tasted them, don't you worry,'

said her father. 'But Grandad will tell you they often used to go hunting for them when he was young. Mind you, there wasn't so much land under the plough in those days, and a lot more rough places where plover and curlew and suchlike could nest. There were many more birds of that sort about than there are now.'

'And now you've gone and ploughed up the Rhos, that'll be one less place again,' said Amanda.

'She's right, you know, Bryn.'

'Oh, don't you start, the both of you,' exclaimed Mr Davies. 'How do you suppose I'm going to make a living out of this place if I'm not allowed to work my own land?'

Amanda didn't know the answer to that, so she went out into the yard to examine the egg better. Even in the bright sunlight it remained dusky and secret. Although it felt so silky, it did not shine like silk, but gleamed softly, as with a hidden inner life. She had a sudden idea.

'How long does it take for a wild duck's egg to hatch?' she asked, going back indoors.

'Twenty-eight days for a farmyard duck,' said her father. 'I suppose a mallard's about the same. Why? Thinking of putting it under a hen?'

'Oh, could I? Mum, haven't we got a broody hen?'

'Well, no, not at the moment. Mind you, I'm sure that speckled bantam is laying out somewhere, but do you think I can find where? She'll probably go broody as soon as she's got a nestful.'

'Blessed bantams,' said Mr Davies. 'More trouble than they're worth. The birds are too small to eat and the eggs are too small to eat, even if you can find 'em, and that you mostly can't. Lay anywhere, a bantam will, except in the proper place.'

12

'If I do find her, could I give her my duck egg to sit on?' asked Amanda.

'It wouldn't work if you mixed them,' said her mother. 'A bantam egg takes a week less than a duck egg to hatch, and she'd just go off with the chicks and leave the duck egg behind.'

'Couldn't I just keep it somewhere warm, like the airing cupboard? Wouldn't it hatch then?'

'I . . . I don't know.' Her mother sounded interested. 'Could she do that, Bryn? Would it work?'

'Oh, aye, it might work all right. It's been done in the past.' Dad always knew about things that had been done in the past. 'But it's not easy. The temperature's got to be just right, and you've got to keep the egg in an *even* warmth – no use cooking one side and leaving the other in a draught. And you've got to remember to turn it over every day, like the mother duck would do. And they do

13

say, with duck eggs, it's best to wet them a bit every few days.'

'Oh, let's do that!' Amanda stared at the smooth greeny-brown egg as though she could almost see the tiny duckling growing and growing inside it. 'I could put it in the airing cupboard, Mum, couldn't I? Please?' To hatch a real live wild duckling out of this magic egg would be so much more special than just to eat it like an ordinary hen's egg.

'We could *try*,' said Mrs Davies.

'The airing cupboard wouldn't be no good,' said Mr Davies. 'Not hot enough. Back of the Rayburn would be better — maybe up a bit, on a block of wood or something, and then well wrapped up. But I think you'd be wasting your time.'

'You said it could be done.'

'I said it *has been* done. But I'd say nine times out of ten, nothing comes of it. It isn't as though you've got a whole lot of eggs.

Maybe if you had a dozen, one would hatch, and the rest would be no good.'

'I'd like to *try*, anyway.'

'Go ahead, then. But I bet by the end of a week either your mother will be sick of trying to cook with that thing stuck at the back of the stove, or you'll have forgotten to turn it.'

Amanda and her mother found a box and laid the egg in it, wrapped lightly around

with cotton wool, and set the box on a thick tablemat balanced on top of a pudding basin; Mrs Davies thought a block of wood might get too hot.

Chapter Two

For two or three days Amanda could not
resist taking the egg out every time she went
into the kitchen, to test whether it felt about
the right warmth and to turn it over. She
would stare at the smooth dark shell, trying
to picture a little blob inside growing into a
duckling.

Then, suddenly, she began to forget about
it. After all, every time she looked at the egg,
it was just the same. Her mother had to
remind her.

'Have you turned that egg today?' she
would ask at supper-time, and mostly

Amanda had to say she'd forgotten.

'I wish you'd find where that bantam is laying – that would be more to the point,' said her father. 'I still see her about the yard, so she's not begun to sit yet.'

'I have looked,' said Amanda. She had, but not very hard. Millie, the bantam, could be laying out under any hedge or patch of long grass, or around any of the farm buildings. Looking for a well-hidden clutch of tiny bantam eggs seemed hopeless.

'You want to watch where she goes,' said her mother. 'That's the best way.'

'But I'm at school all day,' said Amanda. 'And hens usually lay in the mornings, don't they?'

'Not always,' said her father. 'Anyway tomorrow's Saturday, so you can watch her all day.'

Amanda glanced at him to make sure he was joking, and knew that he was from the

17

way his sandy eyebrows had lifted up almost
into his curly hair.

After breakfast next morning she did look
around to see if Millie was anywhere to be
seen, but she was not. Amanda was poking
about among some nettles that grew thickly
where some old sheets of corrugated iron
were leaning against a shed, when she saw
Mrs Morris come into the yard with a jug in

her hand. She knew what Mrs Morris wanted before she spoke.

'Water for the church flowers, is it?' she said. 'I'll fetch some for you now.'

The church was next to the farm, and whoever came to clean it and do the flowers for Sunday usually called at the farm for water.

'Thank you, dear,' said Mrs Morris. 'I'm in a bit of a rush today, what with one thing and another.' Mrs Morris was usually in a bit of a rush, what with one thing and another.

'You needn't wait,' said Amanda. 'I'll bring the water on up.'

Mrs Morris thanked her and bustled off, and Amanda went and filled the jug at the kitchen sink and walked carefully along the lane and up the church path, trying not to spill any. Not that it mattered, but it was a challenge.

In fact, it was Mrs Morris who spilt something. Just as Amanda reached the porch, there was a clatter and an exclamation inside. In her hurry, Mrs Morris had knocked over a whole pile of hymn books and, in trying to catch them, caught the edge of the table where they were stacked, and nearly had that over too. At the same moment there was a loud squawk from above

Amanda's head, and Millie hurtled out past her ears, shouting angrily at the top of her voice.

Mrs Morris was too busy trying to clutch at the hymn books as more and more slipped off the tilting table on to the floor to pay attention to Millie's squawks, and Amanda, as she set down the jug and ran to help her, decided to say nothing about it. But as soon as Mrs Morris had finished and driven off in her old car, she went inside the church and wandered round looking for something tall to stand on and reach the place Millie had come from in the porch. The only thing high enough was the table with the hymn books on that Mrs Morris had knocked over. Patiently Amanda took them all off again, stacking them on the nearest pew, and dragged the heavy table out into the porch. It was quite hard work, but she managed it in the end. Then she clambered up and peered over the top of the thick wall on which the roof rested.

There, among the cobwebs and lumps of fallen plaster and an old rag someone must have once stuffed there, was a nest of twelve pale bantam eggs, glimmering in the shadows. Amanda felt them gingerly. They were smooth and cool but not quite cold, and one was definitely a little warmer than the others. That must be the one Millie had just laid when she was disturbed by the falling hymn books.

Amanda jumped down off the table and began to drag it back into the church, thinking as she did so. She had been keeping her duck egg warm since Monday. Now it was Saturday, and, from the number of eggs in Millie's secret nest, she guessed Millie would very soon decide to sit and hatch them. If she did that in the next two or three days, then Amanda could put her duck egg in with the bantam eggs, and it would hatch just about the same time as Millie's own eggs, if what her father had said about duck eggs taking a week longer than hen eggs was right.

By the time Amanda had put the hymn books back on the table again, she had got it all worked out. As she ran back up the lane, she met Millie coming towards her. When she saw Amanda, she pretended she wasn't going anywhere in particular and started to peck about at the roadside.

'You can't fool me,' said Amanda to her. 'I know what you're thinking about. But it's all right – I won't tell anybody.' Millie put her head on one side and looked at Amanda suspiciously; then she began to scratch in the muddy verge and found something to eat.

Later that day, Millie was to be seen about the farmyard, but next morning she disappeared and was not seen again all day.

'I knew it,' said Mrs Davies, when it was time to shut the hens up that night. 'Millie's gone. I don't suppose we'll ever find her nest now.'

'Not until she turns up with all her family,' said Amanda cheerfully.

'Well, I hope she's found somewhere sheltered,' said Mrs Davies. 'It's going to be a stormy night, it said on the television. It's blowing the wrong way for my old stove too.'

'I know. I can smell it,' said Amanda as they went indoors. When the wind was in a certain direction, it seemed to puff down the chimney into the Rayburn, which her mother stoked night and morning with a kind of coal, and made it smoke into the house. It was a particularly horrid choky sort of smoke, and on bad days Mrs Davies had to shovel out the coal and tip it outside and let the stove go out and not light it again till the wind had dropped. Amanda was about to say something about her duck egg, and what would happen to it if her mother let the stove out; but then she decided not to. Her father came in just then, ready for his tea.

Amanda knew what she had to do, but it was difficult to find an excuse for going out again after tea, as it was raining quite hard, and in any case she could not get hold of the egg while her mother stayed in the kitchen.

However, it grew so smelly from the stove that Mrs Davies gave up any idea of trying to do any cooking for Sunday, and went through into the living-room. Amanda quickly took the duck egg out of its box and put the lid back on, so that nobody would notice. Then she slipped on her wellies and anorak, and ran down the lane as fast as she could, holding the precious egg in both her hands to keep it dry and warm.

When she got to the church, she took off her anorak and wrapped the egg carefully in it, swept the hymn books on to the floor and tugged the table into place. Then, clasping the egg carefully, she clambered up and peered over. She was greeted by an angry throaty noise and found herself looking into Millie's fierce eyes at uncomfortably close quarters.

'It's all right, Millie,' she said nervously, and put her hand up towards her, holding the egg. Millie fluffed out her feathers and growled – there was no other word for it.

She tilted her head sharply sideways and fixed the approaching hand with a hard stare.

'Please don't peck me,' said Amanda; but Millie did – very quickly, and not really hard, but it made Amanda jump and she nearly dropped the egg. She put it down hurriedly beside Millie and drew her hand away. Millie sat and stared at her, paying no attention to the egg. A patter of rain smacked down on the roof above, and a gust of cold wind blew up under the eaves.

Amanda plucked up her courage. There was no point in having kept the duck egg warm all this past week only to let it go cold now while Millie made up her mind whether to tuck it under her wing.

'Nice Millie,' said Amanda, and with her left hand she gently scratched the back of Millie's neck. She could feel Millie's warm and stringy skin under the bristling feathers. The hen clucked in a surprised sort of way, but she must have felt soothed, because she grew a little smaller as she let her upraised feathers settle around her like a cloak.

'It's all right,' murmured Amanda, 'I'm not going to take your eggs away.' This was not exactly true, because as she carefully slipped her right hand, holding the egg, under Millie's wing, she could feel that the whole space under the little bantam was entirely filled with her own eggs. There was nothing for it but to take away two of the bantam eggs. Well, they collected and ate Millie's eggs all the rest of the year, and Millie would never know she had two less.

'It will be much more interesting for you to have a duckling, anyway,' said Amanda. Millie did not seem to think so, because she suddenly roused herself and pecked the hand again, quite hard this time.

'Ow!' cried Amanda, and dropped the two eggs. They fell with a smack on the tiled floor below. She climbed down off the table and looked sadly at the sticky mess of egg and shell splattered all over the floor. She would have to clear it up somehow, or the first person to visit the church would look around to see where the eggs could have come from, and Millie's secret would be discovered. She found a rag in the little room where cleaning things were kept, but the floor was still rather a mess when she had finished, and it was by then too dark to continue.

Luckily, no one was likely to go into the church before the end of the week, and Amanda had a good chance to clean up properly three days later when her father was away at the market and her mother had to stay on late at school. It was just as well she had plenty of time, because it took her ages to scrape off the dried-on egg which she had smeared all over the floor in her first effort with the rag; and then she had to drag the table back and replace all the books. She climbed up first, though, to check that Millie was still there and still sitting on the duck egg. All was well, and Amanda decided, as she tugged away at the table, that she would have to try and find some easier way of keeping an eye on things. When she had finished putting everything in order, she went back to the farm and wandered round the outbuildings till she found what she wanted — an old wooden box, which she dragged along the lane and up to the church, and tucked away round the corner outside the porch.

Next morning the wind had dropped, but there was a horrible, stale, smoky smell in the kitchen, and it felt cold and dead. Amanda went straight to the egg box at the back of the stove.

'I'm sorry, pet,' said her mother. 'I did try to keep it going, because of the egg, but it was no use. It just went out of its own accord — it won't draw properly when there's a wind from the west.'

'Never mind,' said Amanda. 'It probably wouldn't have hatched anyway, Daddy said. I'll throw it out.' She ran quickly to the door with the unopened box.

'Let's have a look,' said her mother. 'It

could be just warm enough still.' But
Amanda pretended not to hear and ran off
to the rubbish heap round the back of the
buildings.

When she came back, her mother asked
what she had done with the egg.

'I don't want to talk about it,' said
Amanda, which left her mother wondering
whether she really minded about it very
much, or simply didn't care.

'I see the old duck egg's gone, then,' said
her father, a day or two later, when he
happened to remember it. And that was all
that anybody said about it.

Chapter Three

Every few days, Amanda slipped off to the church, got the box out from behind the porch and peered in at Millie. Every time, Millie was crouched low in exactly the same position, half asleep. She didn't look as though she ever bestirred herself to turn the eggs over, and she certainly had no means of wetting the duck egg even if she wanted to. Amanda put a small bowl of water nearby, and a handful of corn. Millie paid no attention to either of them, and a few days later Amanda surprised half a dozen sparrows noisily squabbling over the corn. She remembered her father once saying,

'Wherever there's corn, there's sparrows and rats.' She put no more corn up there; after all, Millie had always managed to look after herself in the past.

Then one day she surprised Millie running about the churchyard, thin and urgent, scratching under the bushes for food as though her life depended on it. Amanda fetched the box and went and stole a look at the eggs. They were warm, but did not look any different from when she first saw them. She carefully turned the duck egg over, and went to watch Millie to see if she returned to them before they got cold. Millie, however, was nowhere to be seen, and while Amanda was looking for her, her mother called her in to tea. Afterwards, when she ran back and stood on the box to peer in, Millie was back on the nest, crouched down and half asleep, looking as though she had never moved.

On Sunday afternoon, exactly three weeks

after Millie had started to sit, Amanda went to look, full of excitement. Millie still sat there, not a chick to be seen. But she was wide awake now and glared at Amanda fiercely, making that low growling noise again. From under her came faint cheeps.

'Please, Millie,' said Amanda. 'Please will you let me see your chicks?'

But Millie just sat tight and growled, and when Amanda put her hand near her, she fluffed up her feathers and looked very angry indeed. The water-bowl was empty, so Amanda took it to refill it, and to fetch some corn and chick crumbs. Millie and her family would have to eat now, rats or no rats. Suddenly, for the first time, she realized that Millie had not chosen such a clever place after all; for how in the world was she going to get her tiny family down from that high wall, with only the tiled floor so far below?

She would not be wanting to move just

yet, Amanda decided, and in the meantime
she must think of a way to help her. Most of
the next day at school she worried about it.
Should she try and catch the chicks and lift
them down? They were likely to panic, she
knew, and could easily hurl themselves over
the edge in their fright. Should she put a
ladder of some sort, so that they could get
down in easy hops? Or pad the floor with
straw or cushions? Maybe the time had come
to tell her parents and ask for their help. Not
now, when Mrs Davies was her teacher, but
back home, when Mrs Davies had become
her mother again.

She decided to tell her the whole story as
they came back from school together, but
one of the other children's mothers turned up
at the end of school wanting to talk to Mrs
Davies, so Amanda ran on home by herself,
unable to wait another minute to find out
what had happened.

She came into the yard and there was
Millie, proud as a peacock, clucking to a
brood of ten pale, fluffy bantam chicks. Ten!
But where was the duckling?

Amanda turned and ran to the church as
fast as her legs would carry her. But when she
got near, she slowed down, afraid of what
she might find. One little dead duckling, neck
broken by its fall on to the floor? Or, worse
still, injured, and perhaps caught by a cat?

There was no duckling on the floor. Shaking with anxiety, Amanda fetched the box and climbed up. How could Millie have moved so soon, bringing all those tiny chicks, with wings the size of halfpennies and quite unable to fly, safely down on to the hard floor? Little balls of fluff, they must have been so light that they almost floated like thistle-down. But a duckling would have been bigger, more solid, with heavier webbed feet and wide bill. Would it have somehow known that it was not safe to leap out into space as the little chicks must have done? Or had the egg simply been addled, and no little duck ever grown up inside it?

She peered over. There was the old nest, very shabby-looking now, cluttered with stained and broken eggshells. And there was the duck egg. It had never hatched then. It was almost a relief.

Then she saw that there was a hole in it —

a hole, and a crack running from it across the middle of the egg.

Nervously, she picked the egg up to have a better look. In places the crack was quite

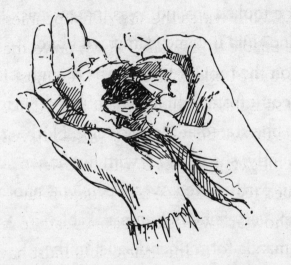

wide, and through it she could see dank, khaki-coloured streaky stuff, more like wet hair than feathers. It was cold, but not very cold because it was quite a warm day. Poor little duck. It must have started to come out of its egg too late, and Millie, with ten active fluffy chicks to look after, had left it to go cold and die. Sadly, and with some disgust because the cracked egg with the oozy grey hair showing through was rather horrid, Amanda put the egg back in the nest.

As she did so, she heard a faint cheep.

She looked around. Was there a chick left behind? Did it come from a wild bird, out on the roof? It sounded as though it had come from right in front of her nose, in the nest. She stared at the duck egg. Nothing.

Gently, she poked it with her finger, so that it partly rolled over. There was another cheep, very faint, but unmistakable.

Amanda forgot her disgust in the excitement, and picked the egg up and scrambled down and out into the sunshine. Peering at the crack in the bright daylight, she could see, quite clearly, a faint movement; the streaky hair moved, ever so slightly, but steadily, up and down, up and down. The little creature inside was breathing!

Holding the egg cupped in her two hands

to give it warmth as well as to keep it safe, she ran as fast as she dared back to the farm, and arrived in the yard at the same time as her mother.

'Look at Millie,' said her mother. 'She's pulled it off again. Ten chicks – that's clever.'

'And a duck!' said Amanda. 'It's not dead! Look!' She held out the egg.

'That's the mallard egg!' said her mother in a puzzled voice.

'Yes,' said Amanda. 'And it's almost hatched – the duckling's breathing. See?' Mrs Davies peered over it.

'May I?' she asked, and took it gently from Amanda's hands and held it in her own.

'It will live, won't it?' asked Amanda. She watched her mother's face. 'It cheeped.'

'I don't know,' said Mrs Davies. 'Warmth, that's the first thing. Back to the Rayburn. Then maybe you can tell me just what you and Millie have been up to.'

'Do you think we should help it out of the shell?' asked Amanda. 'Perhaps it's stuck.'

'It's usually best not,' said her mother. 'But this little duckling will be weak from the cold. You see, it's already cracked the shell almost all round. That needs a lot of strength, and it has to rest between whiles. If Millie left it and it got colder, it would lose the strength to try again.'

'Let's help it,' said Amanda. They were in the kitchen now, by the warm stove.

'First let me get a box,' said Mrs Davies. 'You hold it and keep it warm in your hands while I find one.'

She came back with a shoe box and an old vest of Amanda's. 'We'll put that in the oven for a moment to warm it,' she said. 'Then we can line the box with it.'

The warmth of Amanda's hands were beginning to work. She felt a sudden movement, as though the little creature in the egg were stretching itself against the inside of the shell, trying to push the two halves apart. The crack widened a little but the last unbroken piece held firm, fastened by the tough skin of the inner lining.

'Can't we help it?' she asked. 'It's trying so hard, but it's not strong enough.'

'Perhaps, if we are very careful.'

Amanda pulled at the two halves so nervously that nothing happened. 'You do it,' she said.

Her mother took the egg and very slowly eased one half away. A pair of surprisingly long legs pushed out in quite a strong kick, as if to say, 'I did that, not you.' Mrs Davies took hold of the other half and lifted it and gave a gentle shake. The rest of the duckling slipped out and lay in the palm of her hand. It made a small movement, uttered one cheep and lay still.

'Is it dead?' whispered Amanda.

'No, it's breathing, look,' said her mother.

The duckling lay in a shapeless lump, covered with a film of greyish-looking slime, eyes closed. The streaky hair-like stuff that covered the body clung so closely to the skin that you could see the outline of the tiny bones, and round the eyelid and beak the skin was puckered and bald. It was very ugly.

Mrs Davies took the warmed vest out of the oven and Amanda lined the box with it.

Then Mrs Davies laid the baby duckling in its new cosy nest, and put it on the rack above the stove.

'It'll be warm enough there now,' she said.

All evening Amanda kept going to look at her little duck. It was amazing how quickly it responded to the warmth. Within an hour it was standing up, though very wobbly; and by Amanda's bedtime it had turned into a beautiful picture-book fluffy duckling. It looked twice the size of the moist, limp creature that had been tipped out of the shell, and was covered with soft down the colour of an old walnut. It cocked its head and looked at Amanda with a bright black eye.

'What shall we call it?' she asked.

'How about Bright-eyes?' said her mother.

Amanda studied the duckling carefully, turning the box to get a good view. 'Bright-*eye*,' she said. 'It never looks at you with both eyes at once. Its face is the wrong shape.'

Chapter Four

For a day and two nights, Bright-eye just sat and slept, or occasionally pecked vaguely at the vest. Amanda offered it chick meal and drinks of water, but it took no notice. It never cheeped, not even once.

Amanda grew worried. 'It will die if it doesn't eat,' she said.

'It will eat when it's hungry,' said her father. 'Ducklings and chicks, they don't eat for a couple of days after they hatch; it's just rest they need.'

Amanda was afraid her father might be rather cross about those bantam chicks when he realized she had kept the nest secret all that time, but he just laughed. 'One thing about bantams,' he said. 'They look after themselves pretty well.'

It was no use expecting Millie to look after Bright-eye, though. She might have adopted him if he had been poked in underneath her at nightfall, when she would not have noticed one more or less, but he would never have managed to keep up with the other ten little balls of fluff that zoomed about the yard like bumblebees. Besides, he knew who his mother was: Amanda.

When Amanda came downstairs on the second morning, the duckling began to cheep loudly, and when she gave him some chick crumbs, he pecked at them, eating a few. She put a small bowl of water in the corner of the shoe box, but she had to push his beak into it before he understood what it was for. By the end of the day, however, he

was eating and drinking quite a lot, and the
next day Amanda had to take him out of the
shoe box to give him a drink because he
splashed about and made such a mess.

'Can I take him to the pond for a swim?'
she asked.

'Not yet,' said her father. 'If he gets his
back wet, he'll catch pneumonia and die.'

'But you see tiny ducklings swimming
with their mother on the river,' said Amanda.

'Yes, you do, but that's because when a
mother duck broods over her ducklings, the
special oil she has on her feathers rubs off on
them, and that keeps the water out. A hen
hasn't got that sort of oil – that's why ducks
can swim and hens can't – so if you hatch
ducklings under a hen, you have to keep
them out of the water until they've produced
enough oil to keep themselves dry.'

'How long will that be?' asked Amanda.
About a week, her father thought, but said it

would be best not to try too soon, and then only if it was a sunny day.

It was lucky that the school holidays began at the end of the week, because by then Bright-eye was altogether too busy to leave alone for long periods. Instead of the shoe box, he'd been given a big wooden box on the kitchen floor, which got in everyone's way, and was only put back in the shoe box up on the rack at night, for warmth. Then, as soon as Amanda got home from school, she took him out and let him run about the yard if it was a fine day.

When the holidays started, though, they gave Bright-eye a proper wire run out in the garden, but at first Amanda had to bring him indoors every time it got cold because he had no mother or other duckling to cuddle up against. No doubt about it, he *was* lonely, and it was not long before he was more often following Amanda round the farm, or

sitting in her lap, than he was in his run.
Every time he saw her, he cheeped loudly
and ran towards her, and when she had to
put him in his run and leave him, he
cheeped even more loudly. However, he
would soon settle down and go to sleep if
there was nothing else to do.

He grew at an amazing rate, and ran
about eagerly looking for food from morning
to night. He seemed to be always hungry. It
would be a long time before he could fly,

because it wasn't just his wing feathers that had to grow. The wings themselves were as tiny as buttons when he was first born, and they would be the last part of him to grow to their full size. His legs, though, were unexpectedly long and strong, and he could run very fast indeed. That was just as well, because poor Bright-eye soon discovered that not everything in the farmyard loved him as Amanda did. Millie pecked him smartly when he pushed in among her chicks for food, and the big cockerel chased him when he came too close. He ran, panic-stricken, for cover when the cows lumbered in across the yard, and once he had a narrow escape from a crow who swooped down on what he saw as a tasty morsel with no mother hen or duck to protect it.

Amanda saw the crow fly off as she came round the corner, and for one horrid moment she thought it had taken Bright-eye away in

its beak, for Bright-eye was nowhere to be seen. Then she saw him.

In his fright, he had rushed straight for the nearest bit of cover he saw, and crouched there, quite still, hiding his head under something. The something was the feathery chest of old Meg, the sheepdog, stretched out sleeping in the sun.

Meg was going on for thirteen, and had long since given up getting excited about crows, or ducklings either, for that matter.

When she saw Amanda coming towards her, she thumped her tail and yawned in a friendly manner. Bright-eye burrowed in deeper, between her paw and her neck. Meg lifted her head, gave the duckling a lick or two and laid her head back down again, carefully though, so as not to squash him. Perhaps in her sleepy way she thought it was one of her own puppies of long ago.

So began a friendship which solved everybody's problems.

It did not happen all at once, though if old Meg had had her way it would have done. She began to follow the little duck around, wanting, like a grandmother, to recapture the feeling of something young snuggling up against her, and when she found Bright-eye asleep, she would settle down alongside. At first Bright-eye would scuttle off in fright, calling loudly for Amanda, but one chilly afternoon he decided it was rather nice to have

this warm soft wall between him and the
wind, and he just roused a moment, pushed
up against it and sank back down to sleep.

After that, Amanda began to find that
Bright-eye only came chasing after her when
he wanted food; the rest of the time he
would be quite content pecking about near
the old dog or sleeping between her paws.
Meg no longer worked on the farm — that
was left to the younger dogs. All she did was
sit about in the farmyard and bark, without
bothering to get up, when strangers came.
Looking after Bright-eye was the perfect job,
especially when the next school term started.

Chapter Five

One day when Bright-eye came running
across the yard to greet Amanda after she
got back from school, she noticed he looked
somehow different. Instead of being fluffy all
over, there were smooth patches near the top
of his tiny wings. When she picked him up
and examined him closely, she could see
there were proper feathers, small and flat,
taking the place of the soft cloud of down
that still covered him everywhere else. A few
days later she saw him standing quite close
to Millie. 'How *small* Millie is,' she thought.

'I never realized.' But of course it wasn't Millie who had grown smaller, but Bright-eye who had grown bigger.

After that he seemed to grow bigger every day, and more and more of his down disappeared as the smooth coat of brown feathers spread further and further over his body, until only his breast remained fluffy. He still acted like a baby, though, and ran to Meg for protection whenever danger threatened, crying in his high piping voice. He was rather a noisy duckling. Peep-peep, peep-peep, he went whenever he was startled; and peep-peep, peep-peep, whenever he was hungry; and peep-peep, peep-peep, whenever he saw his friend Amanda. As he grew bigger, the peep-peep grew louder until you could hear it all over the farm. He liked to run about looking for puddles and muddy places, and when he found them he lowered his head so as to get the whole of his beak flat in the shallow water and sucked the water in and out, very fast and rather noisily.

'He's like a vacuum cleaner,' said Amanda to her mother as they watched him one day.

'It's how he gets his food,' said her mother. 'Like a vacuum cleaner sucks in the dust and air together, and then lets the clean air out. He does the same with water and lots of tiny bugs and insects.'

'Yukky,' said Amanda.

'Ducks make very good eating,' said her father, grinning.

'Nobody's going to eat Bright-eye,' said Amanda. But she wasn't worried, for she knew her father was only joking: his eyebrows had gone right up into his sandy hair.

One fine summer day, when the lambing season was over and it was too early to start cutting the hay, Amanda's father decided to do some hedging. He began working on a long straggly hedge that ran down from the farm, across the ends of two fields, to the river. The two young farm dogs leapt around him as he set off with his hook and axe,

excited as always at the idea of going anywhere. Old Meg, perhaps because it was such a fine day, heaved herself up from her place in the sun and wandered along after them. After Meg went Bright-eye.

When Amanda got back from school, no

Bright-eye came peep-peeping to meet her. No Meg basked in the sun.

'Go and ask your father,' said Mrs Davies, who arrived back a few moments later. 'They may be with him.'

'Where is Dad?' asked Amanda.

'He can't be far away. The van's here, and the tractor. I think he said something about doing a bit of hedging today.'

'I remember! Down by the river!'

'Is that where he said? Very likely.'

'You don't suppose Bright-eye would go all the way down there, do you? Supposing he goes in the river, and gets swept away?'

'There's only one way to find out,' said her mother, still sounding rather school-mistressy. She was inclined to go on sounding like that till she had made herself a cup of tea. 'Go and see.'

Amanda ran off down the fields. 'Have you seen Bright-eye?' she asked her father.

For answer, her father jerked his thumb in the direction of the river. 'Having the time of his life,' he said.

'Oh, but he'll get washed away,' cried Amanda, running over. 'He's never swum before.'

Indeed, he never had. For the first two or three weeks, they had been careful not to let Bright-eye get his back wet in case he caught a chill, as her father had warned her, but when he seemed well and strong enough, and Amanda had put out a big pan of water, Bright-eye drank from it but quite refused to climb into it.

'He's not got any other ducks around to show him,' her father had said. 'He'll come, in time.'

But Amanda and her mother had been anxious to see him swimming straight-away.

'Couldn't we give him a push?' Amanda

had asked. 'I'm sure he'd love it once he knew what he was missing.'

'We could try,' said Mrs Davies, and tipped him gently over the edge. Bright-eye shot round the pan so fast he seemed to be running on the water rather than swimming, and bundled himself out over the edge in double-quick time. He shook his little head from side to side so fast that the drops of water flew off him as though he were a miniature spin-dryer. Then he proceeded to preen the damp fluff around his chest and tummy as though his life depended on it.

'Oh, well,' said Mrs Davies. 'Perhaps it's a bit soon.'

'Think of all the fun he's missing,' said Amanda; but there was nothing much she could do about it, and anyway she soon forgot about trying again.

Bright-eye might have been missing some fun during those next few weeks, but he was

certainly making up for it now. He had
discovered a place where an old tree leant
out over the river, its interlacing roots, all
knobbly and twisted, making a kind of ladder
between the grassy meadow above and a flat
patch of sandy mud below which slid gently
into still water. Bright-eye hadn't meant to
climb down the ladder, but, having fallen
over the first step trying to catch a mayfly,
he had found it easier to scramble on down
than to climb back up.

Old Meg wandered over and stood
above, peering down at the little duck for a
few moments, her head on one side and her
ears cocked; then, seeing that he was safe and
happy, she lay down with her front paws on
the edge of the bank, where she could keep
an eye on him.

Bright-eye was indeed happy. As soon as
he had half climbed, half tumbled down, he
began to peep-peep anxiously, finding

himself all alone in a strange place. But in the middle of a 'peep', his beady eye spied a gnat floating in the air above the water's edge. With a quick snap he swallowed it, and was just about to start on another peep-peep when he saw a second gnat, and a third. Then he saw a whole cloud of them drifting lightly along the water and he was much too busy catching them to have time for a peep-peep.

A few yards from the bank the river flowed fast and deep, swirling round rocks and rushing between narrow channels, but here at the muddy verge, protected by the arms of the old tree roots, all was quiet. In the winter, or after heavy rain, there would have been no sandy mud bay; the river rose to the level of the grass, covering all the tree roots and scouring out the earth between them. But Bright-eye knew nothing about that, and thought himself in paradise. Making little webbed tracks which soon filled with water and melted away, he ran to and fro across the mud, stuffing his small tummy with all the tiny flying creatures that hatch and live out their short lives where land and water meet.

In and out of the shallow water he ran, without seeming to notice it, until something caught his eye moving over the pebbles an inch or so below the surface of the water. Down went his bill to catch it, and the cool water flowed over his head and neck. That

was fun. He did it again, moving further out.
Next minute he was swimming and ducking
his head under the water, throwing it up in
cascades of rainbow-coloured drops over his
back. Round and round, back and forth he
swam, ducking and splashing and shaking,
and shaking and splashing and ducking;
never in all his life had he had such fun.

He was still at it when Amanda found him.
Now he was getting bolder, and venturing
further out into the main stream. But he
seemed to know how far it was safe to go.

When the current began to carry him downstream more strongly than he could swim against it, he would steer jerkily towards the shore and come running back up through the shallow water before beginning the game all over again. Every now and again he would cock his bright eye up at Meg lying on the bank, as though making sure he wasn't lost. Once, when he seemed to be drifting so far down that he was likely to disappear from her view, she got up and leaned out over the bank, as though wondering whether she ought to climb down and rescue him. Then, as Bright-eye scudded sideways into the bank and scuttled back up through the shallows, she lay down again.

This time, Bright-eye could see not just Meg but Amanda on the bank. Out he scrambled and waddled across the mud, making a very odd noise. But when he came to the bank, and tried to climb the tree roots, and fell back, he began to peep-peep very loudly indeed.

Amanda climbed down and scooped him up and carried him to the sunny meadow where her father was working.

'He's awfully wet underneath,' she said, 'but his back is quite dry, and his head, but he was going under the water all the time. Not right under, but splashing water all over himself.'

'Never heard the expression "Like water off a duck's back"?' said her father.

'Yes,' said Amanda. 'It's what Mum says in school when we forget something she's kept on telling us.'

'There you are, then.'

Amanda put Bright-eye on the ground and he settled down in the warm sunshine, making the same odd noise he had made before. Meg lumbered over and sat beside him.

'That's the second time he's made that noise,' said Amanda. 'Do you think he's caught pneumonia?'

'No,' said her father. 'But I think you'll have to stop calling it "he".'

'How do you mean?' asked Amanda.

'If I'm not mistaken,' said Mr Davies, 'that was a quack.'

'Quack?' said Amanda. 'Oh! Quack, quack. Bright-eye, are you turning into a grown-up duck?' Bright-eye's bright eye had been getting narrower and narrower as sleep overtook him, tired out after his afternoon in the river, but for a moment, hearing his name, the shield of his lower eyelid slid back and he fixed her with a knowing, shiny, black boot-button of an eye; then the eyelid slid back over, closing out the sunlight, and Bright-eye slept.

'Duck it is,' said Mr Davies.

'I know,' said Amanda. 'I never thought he

was a hen, or a dog. Even if *he* does,' she
added, seeing him cuddled up against Meg.

'She,' said Mr Davies. 'Duck, not drake.'
He went on hedging.

Amanda stared at Bright-eye, then at her
father, then back at Bright-eye again. She had
never thought about him being a she.

'How do you know?' she asked.

'The quack.' Mr Davies laid down the
hook for a moment and pushed the half-
sliced twigs down into a crack, to make a
good strong barrier. 'Drakes don't quack, not
properly.'

'I thought all ducks quacked.'

'They do. Leastways, wild ducks quack. But the drakes don't. They're fellows.'

This was quite a new idea to Amanda. 'What do they do, then?' she asked.

'They make a sort of ... I can't explain exactly. Chchwichk. Something between a whistle and a quack, only not deep, like the duck, nor so loud.'

'Like a duck that's lost its voice?'

'Yes. Higher than a duck, and quieter.'

Amanda looked thoughtfully at the sleeping duck. 'But I don't want Bright-eye to be a girl. I'm used to him being a boy.'

Mr Davies laughed. 'There's precious little you can do about it,' he said, 'so you'd better get used to it.'

Amanda bent down and stroked Bright-eye's head. For a second, the black eye flew open, then slowly closed again.

'Quack,' said Bright-eye sleepily.

70

Chapter Six

Summer passed; autumn blew in with
wrinkled leaves gusting into the porch and
mud so bottomless in the gateway where the
cows stood that Amanda's wellies were not
long enough for her to be able to squelch
through.

Bright-eye loved the marshy ground, and
went whiffling through the wet grasses with
her beak held low and flat, finding all sorts of
things to eat. She wandered far these days,
and sometimes went all the way down to

the river even when nobody else was going. Often, though, Amanda took her when she got back from school.

'After all,' she said, 'old Meg won't go now that Dad's no longer hedging down there, and I'm the nearest thing she's got to another duck.'

That wasn't true, though, as Amanda found out one day. It was raining when she got back from school, and Meg had found her way into the warm kitchen. The working farm dogs were never allowed indoors, but Meg had decided she had earned her bit of comfort now that she was old. A warm hearth, Meg felt, was better than a wet duck these damp autumn days.

So where was Bright-eye? Amanda called to take her down to the river, but when she did not appear she decided to go down anyway and see if Bright-eye had got there first.

As she approached the river, there was a sudden burst of quacking, and a whole crowd of ducks flew up off the river and circled overhead in a ragged line, heads outstretched. Then they flew off upstream – all except one, who circled again and landed back in the river right in front of Amanda.

'Bright-eye?' said Amanda uncertainly, and the duck quacked, and came swimming ashore.

They walked up the fields together. Amanda was thinking hard. Bright-eye seemed to be thinking too; it must have been about the river and the sky, for several times she quacked, and looked back or up. By the second field, she was just thinking about supper, for she ran ahead eagerly to the farmyard.

'Bright-eye has made some friends,' Amanda said to her father and mother over tea. She told them about the other ducks on the river.

'Ah,' said her father. 'We'll have to clip her wings if you don't want to lose her.'

'Lose her?' said Amanda. 'Why would we lose her?'

'She's a wild duck, remember,' said Mrs Davies.

'No, she isn't,' said Amanda. 'She's tame as tame.'

'Yes, but what your mother means is, she isn't a farmyard duck. She's a mallard, a real wild duck, and her mother laid that egg out in the wild. Her mother might have been in that flight of duck you saw. She's got wildness in her blood.'

'You mean, one day she'll leave us and go back to the wild?'

'I reckon she will, unless we clip her wing.'

'What does that mean? Does it hurt her?'

'No, no. You just cut the tips off the long feathers on one wing.'

'And that stops her flying away?'

'That's right. She can fly a little bit, get off the ground if something frightens her; but she couldn't go far. She'd just go round in circles and would soon tire.'

Amanda thought about it. 'Would a fox get her?'

'Well, it's a chance, of course. A fox likes a duck; very tasty to a fox, ducks are. But we've got the dogs around by day, and if she's shut up safe at night, there shouldn't be much risk.'

Amanda put a potato chip in her mouth and ate it before she spoke again. 'I've never seen her fly properly until today,' she said. 'So she wouldn't miss it much, would she?'

Mrs Davies gathered up the plates and stood with them in her hand, considering. She looked as though she were about to say something, but then changed her mind and went over to the sink with the dirty dishes.

'Probably never thought of it,' said her

father. 'Thinks she's a dog, she does.' Up
went his eyebrows.

Amanda giggled. 'I'd like to see Meg
flying,' she said.

'Pretty muddled, your Bright-eye. Can't
decide whether she's a dog or a human
being.'

Amanda was silent, thinking about this.
'She knew what she was this afternoon,' she
said. 'She knew she was a duck. A wild duck.'

She looked across at her mother. 'What do you think, Mum?'

'She's your duck,' said her mother. 'You saved her life.'

Amanda hadn't expected her mother to say that. 'I thought you'd tell me to let her go,' she said.

'I don't think I have to,' said her mother.

Amanda sighed. 'I shall miss her,' she said.

'We kept ducks here in the old days,' said her father. 'Not wild ones, of course. Big fat white ones, for eating. No wild blood in them at all. But I remember, whenever the wild ducks flew over the yard on their way to the river, our old ducks set up quite a racket, quacking and flapping their wings, as though they were thinking of joining them.'

Amanda thought about Bright-eye, head tilted sideways, with her beady black eye fixed on the line of ducks in the sky, her ear directed to catch the sough of their wingbeats; how she would try to fly after them, and just limp round in a circle and drop to the ground again; and watch, and listen, till her eye could no longer pick out the bird specks in the sky or her ear catch the sough of the wings. The wild ducks would circle down to the river, landing one behind another with a splash, as she had often seen them do; and Bright-eye would be left wandering about the farmyard, wondering whether she was a dog or a human being, with a half-thought in her mind that maybe she was something quite different.

Amanda looked at Meg stretched out on the hearth and Meg, catching her eye, thumped her feathery tail on the ground.

'Meg's got the hearthrug,' said Amanda. 'And I've got – oh, lots of things, school and friends and telly and going in the car and sausage and chips for tea; Bright-eye must have the sky and the river.'

Next day, Bright-eye was in the yard
when Amanda got back from school, and she
took her straight down to the river. She ran
instead of walking slowly, so that Bright-eye
with her waddling walk could keep up with
her. She was surprised at how fast Bright-eye
could run, but once or twice the duck took to
her wings and flew low along the ground
and landed ahead of her companion.

On the river, there were no other ducks. Bright-eye played in the water by herself, and found lots of grubs and flies to eat, but when Amanda turned for home Bright-eye followed her at once.

Much the same happened for the next week. Sometimes Bright-eye was waiting for Amanda, and sometimes she was already down in the river. On each of those occasions Amanda thought she might never see her again, but always, when she got down there, Bright-eye was busy enjoying herself, and alone.

Then, one day, she was not alone. The river was quieter than usual because there had been a long dry spell, so it was flowing quite slowly, and as Amanda drew near she could hear a lot of splashing and Bright-eye's loud deep quack, and another, higher sound, a sort of 'chchwichk'.

Amanda crept up quietly behind the old

tree and peered between a fork in the trunk.
Bright-eye was scudding round in small
circles, nodding her head to and fro,
sometimes dipping her beak right in the
water. Swimming near by was a handsome
wild drake, with a green head as glossy as a
holly leaf, wings like peeled birch-bark,
shining grey and silvery-white with a patch

of jay-feather blue in the middle, and a curly dark tail. To and fro he swam around Bright-eye, every now and again standing right up and treading water and flapping his wings. Then he would fly off a little way, only to come whooshing back through the water to settle by her side. She would dodge away for a moment, as though nervous; then back she would come, nodding her head, as if to say, 'You're not like Meg and you're not like Amanda; but I think you're rather like me.'

Amanda wasn't very comfortable behind the tree, and as she tried to change her position she must have attracted the ducks' attention. With a startled 'chchwichk' and a furl of ruffled water, the drake was up and away. Bright-eye paused a moment, and then followed after him; but even while Amanda was saying, 'Goodbye, Bright-eye,' she turned and came down on the field a few metres away.

'Don't you want to go with him?' Amanda said. But Bright-eye just ran up to the farm for her supper.

Next day, though, Bright-eye was gone. Gone from the farmyard, gone from the river; nothing.

Amanda wished she had seen her go. 'You don't think a fox has got her, or she's been run over?' she asked her father.

'No, no; she'll have gone with the other ducks. I saw a whole line of them earlier today, leaving the river and making off up north.'

'Why would they do that?'

'Well, the river's very low, and the weather's warm. They'll be looking for somewhere fresh to find food – up the Wye, maybe, or the Elan reservoirs. They'll come back, most probably, after rainfall, or when the weather gets colder. Then, when it gets really cold, they'll move on further south again, like as not. Ducks are like that. They don't go far, but they keep on the move, all through the autumn and winter.'

'What happens in the spring?'

'They mostly make for where they've been born, to lay their eggs.'

Every day that week Amanda ran down to the river to see if the ducks had returned, but then the weekend came and she had other things to do, and by Monday the weather was so horrid she just went straight indoors and turned on the television. It was nearly a fortnight before she went down to the river again.

It was in roaring flood. Thick yellow-brown waves chased each other between the trees lining the banks; the flat muddy place where young Bright-eye had first played was deep beneath them, and the water sucked and gurgled through the tree roots, washing out the young plants and moss that had thought to make a home there during the summer months. A line of dead leaves and twigs lay in curves along the meadow itself, showing that the river had been even higher and had lapped over the edge of the banks themselves. A little lower down, where there was a dip in the field, it lay in a pool of floodwater still, and here a flock of ducks suddenly rose up, quacking noisily, disturbed by the arrival of Amanda.

They circled, as ducks do, looking warily at Amanda. Some then flew away downstream, but some, perhaps thinking they had seen her often before and she was not a very frightening figure, settled back down, led by one brown duck who seemed less alarmed than any of the others.

Amanda walked a little nearer. The other ducks — all brown, like Bright-eye — swam to the far side of the pool, and Amanda stood still, afraid they would fly off again.

'Bright-eye?' she said. The single duck swam closer, head cocked sideways, the one bright eye fixed on the girl. She would not get out on to the grass, however; she stayed swimming along the edge.

'Come on, Bright-eye,' said Amanda coaxingly. She walked a little nearer, bending down and holding out her hand. 'Quackety, quackety, quackety.'

Suddenly the other ducks took fright, and rose up off the water with a great swoosh and much quacking. It made Amanda jump, and Bright-eye, too. With a startled quack she rose into the air, flying past the girl so closely that Amanda ducked from the passing wing-beat. Then she swung round and followed the other ducks. Away they flew, not circling this time, but in a straight line down the valley, getting smaller and smaller until a wooded hill hid them from Amanda's sight.

When Amanda got back to the farm, old Meg was standing hopefully outside the back door, waiting for someone to open it so that she could slip indoors.

'Meg,' said Amanda sadly, 'we haven't got a pet duckling any more.' Meg just wagged her tail and lumbered off to lie down in front of the fire.

Amanda's mother was laying the table for tea.

'Next spring,' she said, 'perhaps you'll find yourself something else.'

'Next time,' said Amanda, 'I'd like it to be something we can keep for ever.'

'How about a baby brother or sister?' said her mother.

'Do you mean that?' Her mother nodded. Amanda stood still, thinking about it for a few moments. 'That'll do,' she said at last.

Chapter Seven

'Amanda Davies, are you paying attention? Or are you just admiring your reflection in the window?'

'Neither, Mr Evans.' Several children laughed, and Amanda realized she had said the wrong thing. 'I mean, yes, Mr Evans, I was paying attention.'

Mr Evans was new, and young. He had come to teach Amanda's class because Amanda's mother was too busy at home looking after three-week-old William. Much else had happened since Bright-eye had flown away down the river, apart from the arrival of William. Bonfire Night, the Carol Service and Christmas, of course; then the village party, and the trip to the pantomime; then snow, and sliding on the ice in the playground, and fingers burning with the cold inside the snowball-dampened gloves. Then a lot of rain, washing the mud out of the field gates and into rippling patterns across the lane where Amanda now walked by herself to school, and where she could stop and jump, leaving wellie patterns in the mud. Lately she had not wanted to stop for anything, but ran along as fast as she could, because a thin cold wind kept blowing. She didn't like it at all, but her father said it was good to get the cold weather over before the lambing started, and it would dry up the fields for spring ploughing.

Mr Evans was making his way towards Amanda to look at her exercise book. Amanda smiled, laying her arm across the empty page and pointing out of the window.

'That's my father ploughing that field out there,' she said. 'Did you know my Dad was a farmer?'

'Yes,' said Mr Evans. 'Can I see your work?'

'He only ploughed it for the first time last year. Before that it was all rushes. Then, *last* year, he grew roots for winter feed, but they didn't do very well; this year he's ...'

'This year he's putting it back to grass again.'

Amanda checked in mid-flight. 'How d'you know?'

'My Dad's a farmer too. There's not much else you can do with a Rhos like that, except winter feed and grazing. I hope he's leaving a bit of it rough for the wild life.'

'Yes,' said Amanda. 'I hope so too.' She had suddenly remembered that it was there, in the Rhos, that her father had ploughed through the duck's nest last year. She had scarcely given a thought to Bright-eye for months. Now it all came rushing back.

'*Thank* you,' said Mr Evans, slipping the exercise book from under Amanda's arm. 'I thought as much.'

'How was school?' asked her mother when Amanda got home. She was changing William's nappies.

'All right,' said Amanda. 'I was kept in at break.'

'Why?'

'Oh, nothing much. Mum, can I go and find Dad, straightaway?'

'When you've changed.'

'I didn't know he was going to start on the Rhos until I saw him out of the window. I want to remind him to leave that rough corner again.'

'He said he would – it wasn't worth trying to plough it anyway,' said her mother. 'Still, you may as well go – it's a lovely afternoon.'

A few minutes later Amanda was trotting back down the lane in jeans and wellies, munching a biscuit. She climbed a gate, cut across the home field between the cows, too busy snatching at the thin spring grass to pay much attention to her, down across the plashy dingle, skirting the real marsh where the alder trees grew, and out on to the Rhos.

It was all right. Her father was up at the top end of the field, but he had already ploughed the part near the rushy corner and had left it quite alone. Indeed, the rushes grew there more thickly than ever. She waved at her father and waited till the old tractor worked its way down to where she stood. Her father leaned out of the cab.

'You want to take a look in that patch of rushes,' he shouted above the engine noise.

'Why? Is Bright-eye's mother nesting there again?'

'Not Bright-eye's mother. Leastways, I shouldn't think so. Go and look – only be careful how you tread. Far corner – near those bushes.'

Amanda ran across the field. The first part was sticky and slippery where the sheep had trampled all through the winter, nibbling at the turnips where they grew. Then she came to the part which her father had ploughed that morning, and had to stride from the crest of one newly turned swathe to another – every third furrow if she stretched. Then she came to the rough part, all tussocks of dead grass and clumps of reeds. At first she jumped from one clump to the next, for the ground was marshy in between, but nearer the edge where the blackthorn grew in a spiky tangle it was much drier. She crept along carefully, peering in and around every tussock and clump of reeds, finding nothing. She was standing still a moment, wondering where to hunt next, when she had the strange feeling that she was being watched.

Without moving her feet, she looked from side to side. There! A sudden movement. A bright, black boot-button eye blinked. Amanda stared at the spot. Was it an eye or a drop of water glistening in the shadow? It blinked again.

The eye was only a metre from Amanda's wellies. 'If I move,' she thought, 'it will take fright and fly off.' Then she remembered what her father had said. 'Not Bright-eye's *mother* – leastways, I shouldn't think so.'

'Bright-eye?' she said. And then, very

softly, 'Quackety, quackety, quackety?' The eye shifted, as though the head tilted, and from the reeds came a deep quack.

Amanda stepped right up and peered over. There, half hidden by an arch of last year's dead reeds, sat a duck – surely it was Bright-eye? Her head was twisted half over her back so that she could keep Amanda under the gaze of one intent black eye; she made no attempt to fly off.

'Hello, Bright-eye,' said Amanda. She moved round so that Bright-eye could look at her more comfortably. Bright-eye wriggled a little, as though making herself comfortable in her shallow basin of dry grass and reeds, and quacked, quietly, once more. She did not seem at all afraid.

Amanda bent forward, very slowly, and stroked the smooth brown head. Then she slipped her hand down and felt carefully under the duck's body. Her fingers touched

one, two, silky warm eggs; but Bright-eye's
tail feathers had spread out fan-shaped, a sure
sign that she was anxious, so Amanda drew
her hand away, stroked her once more on the
head, ending up with a little scratch at the
top of the neck, just as she once had done
with Millie. Then she stood up.

'Clever Bright-eye,' she said. 'You know,
we've got a new baby, too. I'll come up
sometimes, and tell you about him, and
perhaps you'll let me see your babies too
when they hatch.'

Then she ran home for tea.